JUMPING J(

And Other Poems for Little People

Written by Glennyce Eckersley

Illustrated by

Patsy Allen and Gill Smith

Designed by Charlotte Aspinall Edited

by Rachel Eckersley

Copyright 2018

Published by Crimson Cloak Publishing

ISBN 13 - 978-1-68160-739-9   ISBN 10 - 1-68160-739-5

Library Information

Eckersley, Glennyce

Jumping Jonny

1. Juvenile Fiction   2. Poetry   3. Illustrated

4. Rhyming

These poems were written many years ago for three special little boys named Jonathan, Daniel and Rob Greenberg. Recent additions have been inspired by Matilda Potten and Alfie Bannister.

CONTENTS

JUMPING JONNY

A world away where skies are blue
I met a bouncing kangaroo
He bounced all day across the plain
And jumping Jonny was his name.

He nibbled leaves and pretty flowers
Whilst jumping through the merry hours
But sad to tell he had a plight
Poor Jonny's problems start at night.

When snuggling down inside his bed
With woolly night cap on his head
Plus blue pyjamas warm and cosy
But gosh how chilly are his toesies!

He searched and searched in all the shops
To purchase winter sleeping socks
They sold them for a cow or pig
But Jonny's feet were far too big!

Poor Jonny wrapped them in a towel
When winter winds began to howl
But that unwound or so I'm told
And Jonny's feet were once more cold.

Hot water bottles, still too small
They did not really help at all
Poor Jonny cried "what shall I do?"
My dear old feet are turning blue!

He bought a fleecy sleeping suit
Which all his friends thought rather cute
But then, as feet are prone to do
They split the seams and poked right through.

One night at last he cried "that's it
Why I shall buy some wool and knit
I've found the answer to my plight
I'm sure to have warm feet tonight."

So Jonny clicked and sang a song
From dawn to dusk the whole day long
The world for Jonny then was sweet
Because at last he had warm feet!

OLIVER SPRAT

Here is a tale about Oliver Sprat
A most unusual kind of cat
A marmalade yellow when looking his best
Four white paws and a snowy white chest.

Oliver Sprat is bright as a button
Never eats pork, roast beef or mutton
He only will dine on his favourite dish
Which, wouldn't you know, is freshly caught fish

By night he strolls beneath the moon
But takes a nap in the afternoon
Some days, I'm told, he feels aloof
So spends all day upon the roof.

One day he'll be a movie star
And folk will come from near and far
To hear the tales of Oliver Sprat
A most unusual kind of cat

WISHING

If I lived in the Arctic
It would be rather nice
To own a handsome husky dog
And build a house of ice.

I'd love to live in China
And drink green china tea
And wear kimonos made from silk
What fun all that would be.

Ah but what if I were Russian,
I'd wear a large fur hat,
And ride to school by sled each day
Now what do you think of that?

If only I were Spanish
Now you may find this weird
But I would dance with castanets
Whilst all the ladies cheered.

Now Switzerland would suit me well
With all that lovely cheese
What fun to climb the mountain tops
And yodel if I please.

I'd love to live in Africa
Beneath the blazing sun
I'd ride upon an elephant
And feed him current buns.

Let's not forget Australia,
Just think what I could do
I'd throw around a boomerang
And ride a kangaroo.

But when the days are chilly
And we've crumpets hot for tea
If spread with jam and honey
Then I'm jolly glad I'm me!

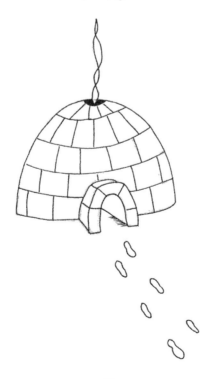

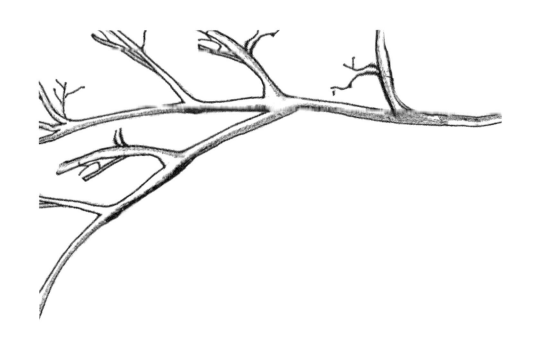

THE FLEA

There once was a flea
Lived high in a tree
He was ever so wee
And would smile down at me
But I had to stare
Very hard in the air
To make sure he was there
Yet by remote chance
His first name was Lance
And he once did a dance
But it started to rain
And I shouted in vain
Would you please dance a reel?
But so wet did he feel
That he turned on his heel
And was gone!

FAVOURITES

My favourite fish is a Skittergee
For he does not live way down in the sea
Where folk cannot see him, my goodness not he
He lives on a mountain and walks on his fins
And when he feels happy
He sits up and grins.

His scales are superb

From doh up to doh

He can sing "Old MacDonald" and "Hunting we go"

He rarely feels home sick

Because of the pills

Which he keeps in a pouch tucked under his gills.

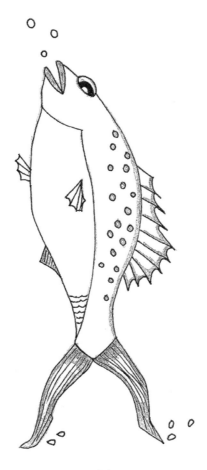

My favourite bird is a pink tailed Kush
Who lives in a treehouse
Way out in the bush
His special food is raspberry bar
Which he makes every day in an earthenware jar

My favourite animal's known as a Fong
He never could bake
Or sing a good song
But he stands six feet tall
With green stripes on his chest
And believe it or not folks
I like him the best.

TOM AND ME

If all the seals in the sea
Were on an island three by three
There'd be no room for Tom and me
So that's a sight we'd never see.

Imagine if all elephants
Placed side by side their mighty flanks
Well what a super sight to see
Alas no space Tom and me.

Now should the schools of whales galore
Form mile long rows of two by four
We could not sail a boat at sea
So we would miss them Tom and me.

Imagine monkeys score on score
All sitting on the jungle floor
With hundreds hanging from each tree
And no spare branch for Tom and me.

It's most unlikely, I'll admit
That all these things should happen yet
But should they ever come to be
We're sure to miss them Tom and me.

MY FRIEND

I have a friend - now please don't laugh
For she's a very tall giraffe
She does not live inside a zoo
Nor on the hills of Timbuktu
My goodness that would never do
But in my garden is a shed
With large roof windows for her head
So when the sky is bright and blue
You'll see her pop her head right through!

And when the sky turns dark from light
She settles down and feels just right
But just before she goes to sleep
It's then she often takes a peep
As in the moonlight clear and bright
I wave to her and shout "Goodnight"
And when she smiles it feels like bliss
So I will grin and blow a kiss.

Now when it's time to wake again
She stands beneath my window pane
So happy we can go outside
I laugh as down her neck I slide

We gallop off towards the park
Where children play, and doggies bark
We wade in streams and through the trees
And my friend nibbles on the leaves.

Lunchtime comes and we will stop
To buy a sandwich from the shop
She reaches to the highest shelf
Where I could never go myself
And at the checkout there is no queue
For people part and let us through
We have a picnic by the lake
With sandwiches and carrot cake

Eventually it is time for tea
My friend is very kind to me
As on her back she lets me ride
And I smile down so full of pride
Now when she eats she's never rude
Politely eating all her food
so very happy to be fed
And through the window pops her head.

At last once more it's time for bed
And off I go, a sleepy head
But knowing as I close my eyes
My friend is waiting when I rise
Another day for me to spend
So happy with my long-necked friend.

ALFIE'S DRAGON

When sitting in his bed one night
Poor Alfie had a dreadful fright
For in the corner by the stair
A dragon sat in Alfie's chair.

He grinned with teeth so large and yellow
He really was a scary fellow
But Alfie did not find this funny
And shouted loudly for his mummy.

Now mummy came and she was cross
She showed that dragon who was boss
The problem here she cried with rage
Is dragon slipped out from his page.

He knows he should not leave his book
She said to Alfie take a look
The book was open on the floor
With empty pages there galore.

But then the dragon hung his head
And both his cheeks had turned bright red
I am oh so sorry then he cried
I promise to go back inside.

I did not mean to leave my book
I simply thought I'd take a look
Alfie's room is clean and bright
I thought I'd stay for just one night.

Alfie then began to smile
And asked if he would stay a while
The dragon said that would be grand
Then I'll go back to Storyland.

When daylight came to lift the gloom
The dragon flew around the room
And giving Alfie one last look
He settled in his story book.

Alfie's mummy shook her head
And lifted Alfie out of bed
A gentle dragon we have met,
Now that's a night you won't forget

OBI

Obi is a tortoise who lives inside his shell
We often think he's smiling but it's very hard to tell
And when he moves he should be slow
But here's what we find frightening
If he climbs from his garden pen
He moves just like greased - lightening!

One sunny day he wandered off
And feeling very chuffed
He found himself in traffic beside a big red bus
The driver smart and careful
Began to slow right down
Whilst asking people on his bus "does Obi live in town".?
"He lives right there" a lady cried "at number 134
I'll pick him up and take him home
And knock upon his door".

His mother gave him such a stare
So shocked to find he'd gone
She made him promise then and there
To stay home from now on
No treats for you tonight, she said
And poor old Obi shook his head.

It's fair to say that from that day
He's been as good as gold
He never leaves without his mum and does as he is told
He knows that roads are dangerous
So he's a careful chappy
And we must learn from Obi and all stay safe and happy.

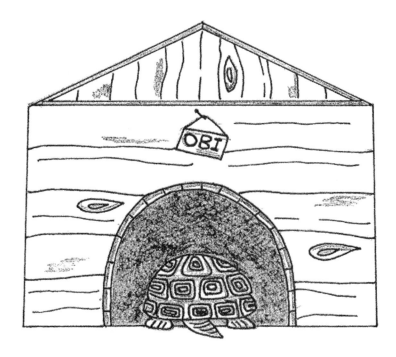

The End

Thank you for reading this book. If you enjoyed it, please consider leaving a review whenever you purchased this book. A review helps an author's book and is greatly appreciated.

AUTHOR

Glennyce Eckersley

Originally science-based, Glennyce worked in a medical research laboratory. In the sixties she worked and lived in Los Angeles and San Francisco for three years. She is the author of fifteen books but this is her first one for children. A regular broadcaster on television and radio, she is also a magazine columnist. Married with two daughters. she lives in Manchester, UK.

ARTISTS

Patsy Allen

Sculpting for many major companies, Patsy has enjoyed huge international sales and exhibits her artwork and sculptures at galleries nationwide. Their children's books, "The Rainbow Scarecrows," sold more than a phenomenal 640,000 copies worldwide. Patsy was commissioned by Gorton Monastery in Manchester to paint St Francis in recognition of his 800th Anniversary. Sky Television has featured Patsy's Angels in their programme, "Real Lives – Angels."

Gill Smith

Since graduating from Art school Gill has become an experienced artist in many different mediums. Pottery, Stained glass and photography amongst them. Her first love is illustration however, and has been delighted to work on her mother's book of poems. Gill works as a laboratory manager, is married and lives in Manchester UK.

Printed in Great Britain
by Amazon

62412702R00031